"The Baker Street Detective 2"
STRANGE TIMES

John Pirillo

Copyright 2022

Table of Contents

Ms. Hudson's Diary

A strange thing on a stranger day
Came to pass that morning.
Few who passed could recall
That time of mourning.
For winds did blow
And rains fell
Like hell from the fires of heaven.
They told the man who might have looked
beware the fates that leaven
Upon stranger days.
---From the secret diary of Ms. Hudson

Stonehenge

July 21, 1849, 9:01am

"The different ways in which a civilized person can choose to live their life is as varied as the infinite number of snowflakes designs that Mother Nature has created. Then does it not cause us to pause and wonder at the eccentricity and arrogance of man to think that what he destroys is so special that it cannot be replaced or duplicated?" From the Diary of James Moriarty.

The ancient monoliths lean towards the sky, reaching upwards with hoary fingers of age and magic, causing a faint disturbance in the air that only the gifted can see. Weaving in and out of the giant stones are white birds chasing each other in a merry game of the air that only birds can do.

One of them arrows from the monoliths and shoots past a lone human making its way towards the ancient ceremonial stones.

The lone figure weaves it their way up the path to the monoliths that have stood the test of time for so many centuries. It seems uncertain at times, weaving a bit, then straightening out and continuing a bit further, until

it pauses and then becomes a bit uncertain again.

If one could hear at that distance they might catch the sound of harried breathing, a gasping, almost strangulating clasp for air that just did not seem to be coming fast enough. Someone choking on the very air they needed, struggling to intake what they could not really quite hold anymore.

Finally, the figure reaches the first of the giant stones and reaches out a gloved hand to feel its surface. Almost as if the person were being somehow healed by the process, they steady and proceed towards the next stone and touch that one. This process goes on as a strong wind blew up, tossing the dark gray clouds that have hidden the sun across the sky and revealing the hoary remains of what could have been a lovely day.

The figure looked up for a moment at the almost bloody skies and pauses, as if in reverence, but then as we move closer, we can see blood dripping down from their eyes and that the eyes see nothing, nor have they been ever able to. For there are none.

Hornsley Street

July 21, 1849, 9:05 am

London, England

"I don't quite remember when I first met him now. It has been so many long, long years ago now, but I do remember that he was taller than most, and his face was round and puffy, as if he had taken on some kind of boxing without the proper protection. But despite that evil look that we used to associate with that face at one time, his nature was open hearted and fair. I've never known a fairer man." From the unpublished recollections of Doctor Watson.

A solitary figure works its way up Hornsley Street. A top hat that seems a bit softer than it should tops the head of a graying man. A man whose years have fled youth and hidden in the wrinkled valleys of time gone by. A man whose life has fled him in many ways, and who now seeks a new and better life, though not exactly sure if that will happen.

A horse and buggy winds its way past and the figure nodded to the driver, as if he knew him, but the driver said nothing and passes without acknowledgement.

A strange thing on a strange day.

The solitary figure pauses, as if surprised, then proceeds

further down the street, his eyes roving up and down the flats that occupy the street. He is sure footed and the cobble stones beneath his feet do nothing to slow him down, but instead seem to give him an extra energy to continue, even though he appears to be struggling to do so at the same time he acts as if he were completely normal.

He stops before a lone flat where the numbers 999 float in a nicely carved flat of wood above arching doors, lit by flickering gas lit. He stares at the flat a long time, as if remembering days long gone by, or trying to.

Finally, he gathers what strength remains to him and slowly ascends the flight of twenty stairs to the doors. As he does, we notice that there is something wrong about this man. For each footstep he took leaves a print of blood, and yet we see no blood on any of his clothing. The mystery of this is further enhanced when he knocks on the front door and leaves a bloody handprint.

The front door remains silent for what appears to

be a long time, and then finally a grumbling sound comes from within. The doors swing wide and a young woman, wearing a robe over her night gowns frowns outside.

The solitary figure doffs his hat, and then collapses into her arms.

She screams and the man slides down the length of her robe, leaving it bloody the length of it, then slumps to the top of the stairs, but no blood stains the concrete, nor drips or drains to pool or gather from the fallen man.

Professor Moriarty

"The different ways in which a civilized person can choose to live their life is as varied as the infinite number of snowflake designs that Mother Nature has created. Then does it not cause us to pause and wonder at the eccentricity and arrogance of man to think that what he destroys is so special that it cannot be replaced or duplicated?"

-- From the Diary of Professor Moriarty.

South Hampton

August 19, 1848, 7:00 am

London, England

The footprint hardly dusted the ground with any kind of imprint, but his spyglass was more than champion enough to disperse the glamour of the dust and mire that usually hid such things. He stooped closer, and then dropped to a knee and his right hand, which was gloved in perfect white cloth and then touched the slightly green grime that was mired with the dust of carriages and the flotsam that came off the Thames that time of morning.

"Ronk!" Blared its horn of a nearby freighter. The loud blast did not so much as drew a single glance or movement of this man's face. Puffy and red like a beet from lack of sleep, the eyes were narrowed in on their target and his ears had tuned out everything but on what he was focused. His concentration was superlative and trained by the greatest mind of that day: Harry Houdini. A master Performer and magician of the first quality, if not a bit arrogant at times for the attention it gathered him.

Admit it he did. His perfect memory was not exactly holding

him back either. And since Harry tended to be a bit fast in his instructions, it helped that he could go back into his mind and sort out everything after Harry was done.

"Watson, I believe I'm onto something." He said, rubbing the green grime between forefinger and thumb, careful not to press too hard. "It has the feel of sugar, but the elasticity of a fine pudding."

Watson, who had been standing back, his eyes on the street to make sure no careless driver took their carriage over his friend, holstered his gun beneath his long cloak, and dropped to a knee beside his friend.

"I don't quite see how such rot can be of help." He remarked in distaste.

"Ah, my dear Watson." Moriarty said with a touch of bright humor. "Impeccable observation as always. Just as I can't for the world of me understand why you would hold a gun behind me."

"If you knew London taxi drivers as I you would also have a gun at the ready." Watson growled.

James cleared his throat, then rose slowly to look at Watson. "I will never get used to the customs of your society; I fear."

"But with perfect memory or near perfect." Watson rambled on. "Surely you will master it more quickly."

James grunted in acknowledgement, then indicated the froth gathered in the gutter.

"You see it's not so much what you do see as what you don't. This has been the scene of a dastardly murder and the perpetrator is none other than that brilliant criminal mind we have been pursuing for years now."

"You think so?" Watson asked a bit too drily.

Moriarty glanced at his portly friend. "Watson, you seem a bit off your game this morning. What has happened to create this?"

"Astute observation as usual." Watson replied to a bit too smugly.

Moriarty frowned, and then shrugged. "Have it your way then. You usually do."

Moriarty placed the grime on the tip of a ball of cotton, and

then pressed the cotton into a small test tube he withdrew from his wide cloak. Beneath the cloak were many pockets and secret compartments, in which he kept his various chemicals and crime detection devices. As well as a few well-placed defense mechanisms, which he kept well hidden from strangers, as well as Watson.

It was not that he distrusted his friend, but he knew that uncertainty often worked to the advantage of the certain rather than the other way around.

"I see." Watson sighed, relieved no further attention upon his personal plight was to be sought. "And now?"

"Why now we arrest the good Judge Harrington." Moriarty declared happily, as he took up a cane from Watson's right hand and leaned into it.

"Ah, my back has never been the same since the plunge from those blasted falls." He complained.

"Had you not been so reckless this might not have happened." Watson said with a touch of anger.

Moriarty frowned. "You are still angry with me, after so much time?"

"You cost me years of grief, my friend." Watson declared, a touch of moisture in his eyes. "Had you truly perished, I don't know what I would be doing today. Probably a drunk lost in a mug of ale over his lost memories."

Moriarty started to grip Watson's right shoulder, then shifted to his left, remembering the injury on the right. He gripped it with his white gloved hand. His only good hand these days. "My dearest friend, your emotions serve you well. But at least we are rid of that scoundrel who called himself my worst enemy and the world's greatest villain."

"Oh, he was your worst enemy, all right." Watson agreed. "But not in detective work, but in leading you astray."

"Had I known he was really a man, I should not have been led so far astray." Moriarty stated matter-of-factly.

"Even so, you were."

Moriarty sighed. "Well, the past is done. And a man may be forgiven his shortcomings."

"Yes, but had you been a true man you would have..." Watson paused for the right words in such a delicate statement. "...you would have investigated the nature of your romantic partner a bit more closely before committing yourself."

Moriarty laughed. "My dear Watson. We are in the height of the golden age of her Majesty Good Queen

Mary of Scots, and you expect me to act like a common soldier and grope the woman as if she were an object?"

"I would have." Watson declared arrogantly.

"And that's why I am the better detective of us, for I never assume to go somewhere I am not wanted, and never want what I assume someone else wants."

With those final words he left a very puzzled and confused Watson behind as he tap-tapped up onto the sidewalk, and painfully made his way towards Baker Street.

Watson finally returned to his senses and caught up. "Why the devil won't you summon a carriage?"

"Because the body is unwilling to serve, doesn't mean I should be willing to serve its pleas." Moriarty stated the hint of a grimace on his face as he moved forward. "Pain is a reminder of the gift of life we cherish and the promise of pleasures we might yet have."

"You're insufferable." Watson said, shaking his head, but secretly admiring his friend's fortitude. "I fear that I should have been reduced to a drunken stupor many, many years ago by a similar kind of situation."

Moriarty stopped and gripped Watson's arm. He glared into his eyes. "Don't you ever say that again to anyone. Your moral turpitude will be your undoing yet!"

"And yours, Professor Moriarty, will be the salvation of humanity yet." Watson returned with a smile.

They both nodded their heads, their fight forgotten, and friendship reforged anew.

It had been two years since that fatal plunge from the Reichenbach Falls and James was no longer the healthy man he had been, but with time and the gentle healing that Madame Curie provided with her homeopathic remedies, he might even yet regain the full use of his hand and someday his legs as well.

Meanwhile, he hobbled as the wounded man he was, but his soul soared with the eagles.

James Moriarty

August 19, 1848, 9:07 am

London, England

"The way in which I live with my life and the pain I have to carry every waking moment is to focus on those things which I can prevent from happening. Since my horrible accident fighting with my arch nemesis and my plunge towards what many assumed was my assured death, I have learned a great humility from my body. While not the most handsome of men before, even more less so now, I carry within my soul the spark of humanity that divinely lit all mortals when they grasp for more than they are to become; more than they can be."

--From the Diary of James Moriarty.

221 B Baker Street

August 19, 1848, 9:07 am

London, England

Ms. Hudson stared at the setting she had placed on the dining table for James and Watson, and then plucked at her right eyebrow, a sure sign of uncertainty. Had she forgotten something, perhaps a lighter linen, the one with the lacy butterflies would have been better?

James took the pipe from between his lips and smiled at her. "The silver will do fine, Ms. Hudson."

Watson added with the hint of a smile on his lips. "And the lacy one with the butterflies is still in the laundry."

She gave him an approving look. "You are so, so right, good Doctor. I'd better finish my laundry in time for dinner."

She raised her left eyebrow, and then nodded her head, causing her long brown hair to bob behind her as she hurried off into

the small kitchen of their apartment to tend to the meal.

She came back in as if having forgotten something.

James shook his pipe at her. "Yes. The lacy linen with butterflies will do nicely for dinner."

She blushed and withdrew again, causing both men to chuckle. They both loved the woman in their own ways.

Watson mused for a moment upon her withdrawal. He noted that the streaks of silver that had been appearing in her hair were becoming less. He shrugged. Women will always find a way of altering their looked to please a man. And each other he added with a grin.

His affection for her had only grown deeper over the years, though never completed. He just could not bridge that final gap of emotional void that the loss of Holmes and his Soo-When had created. Maybe he never would. He was a healthy man if a bit overweight at times. He put on weight. He took it off. When he was on adventures, he lost the weight. When he returned, he put it on. And at that precise moment it finally came to him why that was.

"Ms. Hudson!" He exclaimed rather loudly.

She popped into the sitting room a bowl in her hands. "Something wrong, Doctor?"

He smiled at her. "No....I... uh..." He waved his hand in a meaningless gesture. "I uh...just wanted to tell you how grateful I am for the care and..."

"And what, Doctor?" She asked, a hint of expectation in her voice.

"For your good care and your complete sense of what the womanly thing is to do for a man." He finished, angry at himself and her for trying to coax it out of him, that which they both knew and felt, but were too wound tight to let go of and speak. He had also stepped on the toes of her womanhood. She was very much involved in the new Women's Rights Movement, and he could not have ever said anything worse to her at that moment.

Her chest fell for a moment and her smile vanished, then she perked back up and smiled again brightly. "Oh, you're so welcome. John." She said as she vanished.

James gave him a look and smiled. "John, hey?"

"Oh, behave yourself." Watson snapped at him. "She's just being friendly as always."

"Of that I'm certain." James answered, his grin not leaving for a moment. "But I think your Woman's Right violation is going to cost you severely."

"I do so hope not. It's trouble enough as it is to keep my wits about me without struggling with the concept of women doing anything they freely desire."

"But Madame Curie and Miss Harker have been doing so for all the years we've known them."

"Yes. Just so. But they are not women."

James gave Watson a wag of his pipe. "Oh, you better pray they never hear that one, or they shall make Ms. Hudson's anger look like a puddle in the middle of a tsunami."

"Exactly." Watson admitted with a sour tone. He was so distracted that he could not gather his thoughts in any kind of coherent manner.

Watson sat on the window seat of their flat, overlooking Baker Street. "Have you ever wondered, Professor, what our lives might be like were we different people today?" He asked.

James tapped the stem of his pipe against his right temple, then said. "Oh, you mean if I were not a detective?"

Watson turned to look at his companion. "No, if you were the master villain you fought at the Reichenbach Falls."

James laughed so hard he accidentally spilled his pipe contents into his lap. He laughed harder, even as it scorched his leg. He quickly, removed the remains to the floor and stomped on them, much to Ms. Hudson's dismay as she re-entered with a tray of sandwiches.

"Oh, my dear God in heaven, you've ruined my good carpet!" She exclaimed.

James rose and took her tray as she dropped to the floor to exam the ruins he had created.

"I'm sure you'll find the majority of the damage is to my personage, rather than to your beautiful carpet."

She rose, and then smiled quickly. "I'll be right back."

She came back quickly with a small whisk broom and pan and cleaned up the carpet. Satisfied with the results, she exited the room.

James sat down and helped himself to a sandwich. "I so

love her cucumber sandwiches."

Watson frowned. "Again?"

"What's wrong?" James asked. "Is she punishing you?"

Watson's cheeks reddened. "Why ever would she be tempted to do such a foul thing, sir?"

James laughed. "Well, first when she entered the room, there was not one look to you. Second, she made it a point to put the sandwiches next to me. Third she never once asked what condiment you would like on your sandwich. She always does, except for this day. And fourth you refused to even look at her. So, you missed her look of triumph. Elementary, my dear chap, to quote an old friend of yours."

Watson fumed a moment, and then smiled. "Ah, how well you know us." Pause. "And him."

He jerks about. "Did you say triumph?"

James shook his head and waggled a finger. "Quoth the Raven, 'Nevermore.'"

Watson sighed. "You've learned a lot from my old friend."

James nodded. "Your journals of his work have been nothing less than astoundingly uplifting to me. Were I to meet the man on the street I would recognize him at once and call him friend. Our friend."

"Unfortunately, were he alive now." Watson shot back. "He would recognize you immediately and put a bullet between your eyes."

They both broke into a thoughtful laughter, tinged with remorse. James thought back again to the woman he had left behind so many years ago.

Watson thought back to Soo-when and her almond eyes set against the blush of her golden skin.

Both men felt a great sadness for a moment, but neither were cynical about life or their lives. So, life went on. And James continued his not-so-subtle attempt to help his friend with his emotional distress.

James ate another bite of his sandwich, then reached for a small cup of tea to his left and sipped. "So, when are you two

going to finally conclude this comedy of errors?"

"This is not a Shakespeare play, James!" Watson blurted out angrily. "More like a gentle poem by Shelly."

"Dream on, dear chap. Definitely more along the lines of Wagner."

"I abhor Wagner."

"Have you ever read Wagner?"

"Have you ever read Shelly?

James shrugged. "Touché, dear Doctor."

"I rest my case." Watson said with a sense of relief to turn the topic elsewhere at last.

But James was having nothing of it. One thing he had learned about his partner of yeas was his stubborn refusal to face the facts at times, especially when it came to himself.

"Marriage, my dear friend. Honor and truth in a relationship. I for one would love to be your best man, even if I am truly not the best, but the second in her eyes."

"Some jealousy?" Watson asked pertly, turning the lyrical knife about.

"Indeed." James answered. "Indeed." He replied with an amused look on his lips.

A loud thumping came from downstairs. Ms. Hudson hurried from the kitchen and went downstairs. A moment later a man's deep voice could be heard. Moments later footsteps, then Inspector Bloodstone strode up into view, looking all clean and proper.

The man was medium height and wore a badge with a gold title on it just over his heart. He wore a suit two sizes too big and a handlebar mustache long enough to hang a coat on.

As he came into the room, he spotted the sandwiches. "Don't mind if I do." He said, then quickly woofed down two, smacking his lips noisily as he did, then between bites, he remarked. "Ms. Hudson, however, do you maintain these two gentlemen while still being the hub and center of all male standards of beauty and grace."

Ms. Hudson blushed, rushed into the kitchen, and came out with a large cup of coffee. "I just made it."

He took it with a half bow from the waist. "You are a Princess to this humble fool." He told her, his eyes dancing with delight over her figure.

She glowed beneath his ministrations, but a part of her was aware how it affected Watson and so she put on a bit more affectation than she might otherwise have been wont to do.

She kept her back to Watson, who was growing a bit angry over the flirtations going on so he could not see her face, thus causing him even more concern with his imagination working overtime.

She hurried out and came back with a coffee pot and poured more into his cup, making sure that she kept her back to Watson. "Mustn't let this get cold. The blend doesn't taste as sweet."

"I'm sure you would never taste sour, dear heart." He boldly stated.

She gasped a moment, then giggled and poured him even more as he wolfed down the rest of the first cup.

"Why, thank you!" Inspector Bloodstone said, then took a long drink and set the cup down.

"It's nice to have a man who appreciates the value of a woman." She said a bit loudly as she turned to walk past Watson, who still could not see her face, or the smile that blossomed on it. She was working his jealousy like crazy and he did not know it.

What fools we males be! James sighed inwardly. Having seen everything and rightly deduced the point and center of all of it, he was sad, not surprised.

Inspector Bloodstone, however, like most men caught in the webs of a clever woman, had not a clue as to how he was being used.

He turned to James. "We have a case for you."

"I was never under the delusion this was a social call. Not in your nature." James responded. "And how is the good judge

doing?"

"Quite well in his nice new home of stone and metal." Inspector Bloodstone replied. "He wanted me to send his regards, but I don't think a bullet between your eyes would be suitable administration of his warm thoughts."

James nodded. "Such is life."

Inspector Bloodstone sat down, tapped his right foot several times on the rug, and then looked up. "It seems the arrest has raised another and more needful problem."

"Ah." James said. "You mean the mistress?"

Watson and Inspector Bloodstone both gave grunts of surprise.

Ms. Hudson came back into the room, but her eyes were only on James.

Ms. Hudson blushed. "I think I'll be heading back to my cleaning chores." She exited the room and went downstairs, with Watson's eyes following her as long as he could. So much so that he had to rub his neck afterwards from the crick in it of doing so.

James shook his head. His poor friend.

Inspector Bloodstone noticed. "Fighting again, hey?"

"None of your business, sir." Watson declared, his cheeks reddening with anger.

Inspector Bloodstone put a hand up. "Sir, you have my admiration and friendship, please do not set them aside in a moment of emotional peevishness."

Watson sat there stunned. For he had never heard such eloquence from the Lieutenant before.

"My God, Lieutenant." Watson exploded. "James is rubbing off you as well."

Inspector Bloodstone turned to James again. "Even so. Infectious diseases have that nature, don't they? But how did you know this fact I had never revealed?"

Watson nodded in agreement. "And in James Regards, more like an epidemic of cyclonic proportions."

James laid his pipe down and regarded them both a long time. Both men fidgeted under his gaze. But he did not respond to their criticisms, instead choosing a different road to travel.

"Watson, remember when we were on the street, and I found the green grime?" James asked.

"Yes."

"Examined it with the new microscope that Tesla and Edison produced recently. The one that can magnify even electrons."

"Oh, I think it's called an electronic microscope." Inspector Bloodstone said knowledgeably.

"Actually, it's just a microscope." Watson clarified. Tesla and Edison have agreed to not use the word electric anymore unless it pertains to something each of them built together."

"Well did they
or did not they do it together?" Watson demanded.

"On a legal standing, no. But on a private, companionable sort of way, they both contributed."

"Rest my case." Watson said.

"Oh." Inspector Bloodstone added, not sure who had just won.

"Anyway, I did a chemical analysis with my equipment that Tesla designed for me. It was make-up. Which meant a woman. Now I know that some of the upper-class males have been adding make--up to their daily routines, but this one belongs to the Channel line that only women use. Along with the DNA of the good judge, I had to assume there was some commingling of flesh for this to occur."

Watson blushed, as did Inspector Bloodstone.

"You mean..." Inspector Bloodstone began.

"Yes. The horizontal tango is what the cruder members of our sailing class would call it." James went on.

"I see. I see." Watson said, looking away in embarrassment.

Inspector Bloodstone cleared his throat, and then nodded. "Very astute. Very astute indeed. But must you be so graphic!"

"So." James said.

"So." Inspector Bloodstone repeated, and then nodded. "Assume you know who that partner was as well?"

"Yes." James said.

"I also will assume you will promptly forget." Inspector Bloodstone went on.

Watson stood up and shouted. "Are you out of your mind, Inspector Bloodstone? James does not cover up crimes against her Majesty!"

James wiggled his left index finger at Watson. "In this case we have no choice but to protect Her Majesty's good name."

"Oh, bloody Mary!" Watson shouted, and then blushed again. "You're saying that the Good Queen

Mary...that the...oh dear." Watson's face turned even more shades of red than it usually did.

"I'm so sorry, Inspector Bloodstone. I did not. Mean I..." He fumbled to find the right words.

"Don't be," Inspector Bloodstone said as he rose. "We all forget ourselves sometimes. Trust you will not."

Watson inclined his head. "Forget what?" He said with a blank face.

"Exactly," Inspector Bloodstone said, and then exited. "Thanks for the coffee and sandwiches, Ms. Hudson." He cried over his shoulder as he descended, and Ms. Hudson ascended into view.

"Will you two be needing me further this a afternoon?"

James shook his head.

Watson gave Ms. Hudson an expectant look, which she ignored. "Then in that case I'll be leaving for the country."

"Country!" Watson blasted out. He stood up again, aghast at the besmirching of his emotions. "How dare you run away when we are in the middle of a fight?"

"In the words of the good Lieutenant." Ms. Hudson said with a smug smile. "Exactly."

She exited.

Watson started to go after her, but James placed his cane in the good man's path.

"I think fire burns hotter with fuel, then without, dear Watson."

Watson stood there fuming a moment, then bowed his head in shame and reseated himself. He began drumming his fingers

impatiently against his chair. "I think I shall go insane with worry."

"Then fear not. I have just the right thing to feed your frenzy for action."

James leaned forward and told Watson, whose eyebrows lifted higher and higher as James continued.

Doctor Watson

"I have never known a braver soul than my dear companion, James, nor a more compassionate one. Dedicated to the solving of crimes no one else dares even attempt, he constantly amazes me with his fortitude and his generosity. Even in the midst of the most heinous circumstances he has time for a kind word of his opponents, even of his arch nemesis, whom I would kill without the blink of an eye were it my ability to do so." ---- From the unpublished recollections of Doctor Watson.

Good Queen Mary's Royal Coach

August 19, 1848, Noon on the dot

London, England

Good Queen Mary of Scots, and now present Majesty of all Good England, pondered the craziness of her life, as well as the imponderability of it all. How she must always put on the best face, even if an aging one at this time. In her younger years she could stand up before her people and dazzle them with her beauty, but now in her later years her mind was all she had left, and being the smart woman she was, she realized that to not use the tools that the Good God had given her would be to compound her problems and confound her life.

A short woman, still lean in her later years, the dazzle of her blazing red hair still hinted at through the growing tendrils of gray and silver that were sprouting like little monsters about her scalp, she was not old. Nearing her fifties, she had a huge burden on her shoulders that few had. Even Pope Alexander for all the world he had conquered with his faith and spirituality, even he had less of a burden, as the only ones plotting to overthrow him were too busy praying for forgiveness to train in such a plot.

She grinned, raising her silk fan to cool herself. Her stark blue eyes took in everything. She did not have perfect memory like some of those she surrounded herself with. Men of great common sense and courage, as well as gentle ladies. No, she did not. But her memory was more than adequate to the hammer that plunged on the metal of her patience and fortitude on a daily basis.

She wore an exceptionally soft velvet dress, trimmed with the latest sequins imported from the India Islands. She checked them out for a moment and could see miniature Ganesha and Lord Krishna waving from them. She loved the Islands, which is why she had finally given them their freedom without bloodshed.

Her rule of England had nothing to do with conquest but was more of a mothering and protecting one. So, she sat there watching the crowds of pedestrians as they went this way and that way on their errands, hardly noticing her coach, which moved slowly along the main street towards the palace. Once upon a time they would have stopped to gawk and stare. Part of her felt amused at the switching of this passion by her peoples, but another part was angry. Angry that time and age were her enemies and not her friend. She had so much more to accomplish before the Good God chose to take her back to Him. And she loved her people for ignoring her now even as she hated the pressure of aging. She loved them for she knew they trusted her, and she hated the aging because it meant one day, she would no longer be able to help them anymore.

She sighed sadly, then perked up. But even so, she still had a good decade or two left, God willing, and she was going to do as much as she could to liberate the pagan lands about England as much as she could while holding her people safe from harm.

She sighed and leaned back against the plush red velvet cushion behind her head. Her neck was stiff again. She would have to remind her quack doctor to work on it again. He claimed to have found a new technique imported from India that would relax what he called the muscles that supported the vertebrae of her neck.

All that gobbledygook mystified her. And she suspected it did him as well, but he was a well-meaning soul, if a bit baffling at times with his methods. And more importantly, his son was engaged to one of her three daughters, Rosalie, a perky and pretty thing who was from another world at times. Sometimes she told her mother of the strangest dreams, of a young man who loved her so much he was willing to face death for her.

So, the love of her daughter gave her more patience for his pseudo-science, even as mysteriously it worked to relieve some of discomfort, which her good doctors insisted was impossible because of the damage to her nerves in those areas. "Be damned the whole lot of you," she cursed the medical practitioners for their narrow minds. She was the one tinkered with, not them! They still got huge sums of money for not offering her a single peaceful moment that was not dependent on their soporific drugs which she hated taking.

As a Queen, she took her position seriously, not wanting to harm a single soul she was given to protect. Yet, as a human being, sometimes she just wanted the pleasure of slapping an arrogant face or two. But fortunately, this day she was on her way to meet a man whose face, while not the prettiest, was certainly one she would never want to slap. Were she twenty years younger, she might even want to kiss that face, as unhandsome as it was. A man with a brighter light for a soul and mind she had never met. Sadly enough, his face at one time had been very handsome. But the fall...well. That had taken that away from him.

As her coach slowed to take a turn, she felt a weight upon the rider beside her door. She looked over and a very grim looking man stood there. He grimaced at her, and before she could say anything, had managed to open the door and climb inside.

"Glad I could catch you before you went too far." He apologized, pulling off a wig of hair, and sliding off a fake nose and mustache.

James sat down opposite her and smiled. She offered her hand, and he kissed its ring. "It is my pleasure to be at your service."

She smiled, despite her sense of displeasure, at his abrupt appearance. By now she was growing uses to all his disguises and his mechanisms to avoid being discovered, one of which she noted on his wrist.

Upon her glance he eyed the odd sundial like contraption. "It's an invention of mine that Tesla helped me build."

"Whatever in the world does it do?" She asked.

"Tells the time."

"You mean it talks to you!" She exclaimed.

He smiled indulgently. "No, Your Majesty, only that any mind that has the persuasion can read the dials when out in the proper light and tell what time of day it is."

"But what of night?" She asked. "Can it do so then as well?"

"Working on it." He said with a roguish smile.

He leaned out the window. "Watson take us to Wembley Park, I think Her Majesty could use some fresh air and a bit of a walk."

She gave him a shocked look.

He grinned again. "Oh, yes, he's getting way cleverer these days."

Then the carriage sped up and began weaving more quickly through the street traffic, the curses of Watson from above amusing them both as they sat in an amiable silence.

Good Queen Mary of Scots

"Oh, it's easy for a commoner to pick up an axe, a pick, to carve a ditch, to cook and to complain about the state of affairs, but to actually have to live day by day, hour by hour, and even moment to moment with the weight of decisions that can mean life or death for some...that is a weight that can cruelly torture even the strongest of hearts."

-- From the Affairs of Good Queen Mary of Scots.

August 19, 1848. 1:30 pm

London, England

The ancient trees were intriguingly quiet as they leaned against a dull blue sky heavy handed with dropping gray clouds that threatened to disgorge their swollen bellies of an enormous amount of wetness that formed the kinds of rain that came this time of yet. Drenching the earth while the sun shone overhead scorching it at the same time. A very humid and weary companionship at times.

The lawns of the park were immaculate. They had to be as the groundskeepers knew the Good Queen Mary could pop in at a moment's notice and because they loved to see the small children of couples springing happily about, no worry over what might be under or on the lawns that could ruin their dancing, playing figures.

Row after row of heavily cultivated rose bushes ringed small carefully designed bushes that were thick with green leaves tightly clasped together, as if romantically holding on against the world about them.

Even as the party walked along the narrow cobblestone path of the park a light breeze began to stir, and the smell of rain filled the air.

It would not be long now, thought Watson as his eyes danced among the gardening delights of the park, searching, and searching as he discretely followed the Good Queen Mary, Watson's eyes searched right and left. He took his bodyguard duty seriously. And while the Good Queen Mary was an exemplary ruler and had the hearts of the commoner firm in her hands, she was still a target for the ambitious capitalists who hated her so-called welfare state where she saw to it that all children had food to eat, and no one went without food or medical care, except by choice.

Interestingly, the only few who complained were those who had enough to feed, clothe and educate millions, but instead hoarded their wealth for their own sometimes cruel and selfish pleasures. Yes, even a saint has enemies, and while not a saint, the Pope Alexander called her close to one and that created even enemies who were popular leaders in other countries.

So, it is no surprise that he would become a bit jittery when a mother and two children suddenly appeared from the side, trailing a baby cart. Something about the situation seemed, well, uncommon.

He felt, rather than saw something furtive about the way the two children played. It was very unchildlike. Most children have a kind of randomness in their play, but these two seemed almost calculating. At first, he shrugged it off to a missed lunch because of Morality's sudden fetish for speaking to the Good Queen Mary, who was his best friend and provider of clients, but then when the children suddenly veered off track in a beeline towards James, he grasped for his weapon.

"Halt!" He shouted at the two youngsters.

They froze at the tone of his voice. The woman turned around and he saw a man's face, not a delicate feminine one at all. He had been right. Then he saw something else. It was Inspector Bloodstone.

James and the Good Queen Mary paused for a moment to look back, then continued their stroll, both deeply involved in their conversation, which Watson had not a clue what was about.

The two children turned around and looked up and he could see that they were small people. He took a breath of relief and

holstered his weapon again.

He stormed towards Inspector Bloodstone. "You know I could have shot you!"

Inspector Bloodstone grinned mischievously. "An officer of the law is above such violence."

"May I remind you that I am not...an officer of the law." Watson said rather pointedly, pulling angrily on his handlebars.

Inspector Bloodstone bowed his head slightly, and then snapped his fingers. The two small people ran up. "Right and left." He ordered.

They nodded, and then took off to the left and right, paralleling the Good Queen Mary's course. Watson watched a moment in silence, and then swung back to Inspector Bloodstone. "Surveillance on the Good Queen Mary?"

"Not at all." He replied. "Just helping out an old friend."

"James? Your friend?"

Inspector Bloodstone grinned but said no more.

Watson shook his head. "Oh, dear God in heaven. Bloody Mary, do not tell me you too!"

Inspector Bloodstone put a finger to Watson's lips. "Shush. None shall ever hear of this. Understand?"

At that exact moment James turned to look back and winked. Watson knew at that moment that the secret was far from secure and safe but said nothing. He just grunted.

"Well then. Do what you must, but do it away from me, sir." He warned.

Inspector Bloodstone pulled the bonnet over his head down

lower and batted his eyes, then giggled in a girl like voice. "It was so nice to speak with you, kind sir."

Watson wanted to bang the Lieutenant over the head at that moment but resisted the urge. There would be better times than this to encourage is temper.

Inspector Bloodstone

"Give me a pint of the finest ale, a pretty pair of stockinged legs, and the smell of fresh pig on the fire and I am a content man. But give me the pocket change that jingles freely in the clothing of the privileged; give me the hopes and dreams of those who believe they are special and above the law; those I shall inhale and spit out as the swine they are." A quote from Inspector Bloodstone.

221B Baker Street

August 19, 1848. 3:46 pm

London, England

Watson and James swung off the sidewalk and stepped up to their flat. Ms. Hudson was already at the door. She took their coats and hats and followed them up the stairs.

"I rather think the two of you must be starving by now." She said in an overly sweet voice.

"I thought you were off." Watson said a bit more severely than he felt.

She stepped closer to him and spoke. "A manly man would know a woman's needs better." Then she hurried up past him and James.

James looked across at Watson, who seemed both deeply troubled and confused. "Dear Watson, women shall always be the bane of your life."

"Not of yours?" Watson recoiled.

James took it in stride, even though his own heart felt a degree of tenderness. He had been thinking a lot about Rosalie of late, though God only knew why.

"And why is that?" Watson demanded arrogantly. "Play your silly game, since you leave me no other choice."

"Because you understand them as well as you understand your appetite for food. You believe that when it's time to eat, you eat, and when it's time for love, you love, but neither rule is true, nor binding when it comes to the other sex."

"How would you know? You've never been married once." Watson threw back at him.

"And that's just my point, dear Watson." James said with a grin. "You have been married four times."

With that final word he almost flew up the rest of the stairs, while Watson dropped back, humbled by his friend's conquest of pain and deep understanding of human nature and even more deeply troubled than before by his lack thereof and something else he could not quite put a finger on.

Then he realized what it was. His face brightened. Had there been something more he could do than he had to this point in time. Were their worlds so different?

With those thoughts running in the back of his mind, he almost flew up the steps, where Ms. Hudson gave him a surprised look when he swatted her on the bottom as he passed.

"Oh!" She cried out.

A Grain of Truth

"The greatest crime of life is not the one we have committed, but the one we thought to commit, but feared to complete."

--From the Thieves' Guild Headmaster.

121 A Lashley Down Street

August 19, 1848. 6:46 pm

London, England

Inspector Bloodstone poised before the door to his flat, his eyes on the street. Someone or something followed once he left Wembley Park with his side kicks. He did not think it was Watson, because the man was too astute to spy on his friends. Then he frowned. Or was he a friend. Lately, he had been noticing things about Watson that was off the mark. For instance, his not remembering that Inspector Bloodstone would be doing double duty watching the Good Queen Mary, and his earlier invite to Baker Street, where the man seemed overwhelmed by his relationship with Ms. Hudson, who herself seemed a bit off as well.

"No matter." He muttered to himself, and then reached to open his door. As he did, he noticed that his fingernails were bleeding.

"Bloody hell!" He uttered, horrified. "Have I gone and cut myself somehow?"

Then a newsboy walked past. He stopped and looked up at the stunned Inspector Bloodstone. "You all right, mate?"

Inspector Bloodstone gave the newsboy a questioning look. "Why would you ask?"

"There seems to be blood where you have been walking, sir." He replied.

Inspector Bloodstone looked down, and then noticed that his footsteps left footprints of blood, starting at the curb.

"What the..." He cursed. "How did those get there?"

Then his eyes rolled up in his head and he collapsed, tumbling down the steps to the sidewalk, where the newsboy shoved two fingers between his lips and blew a shrill whistle.

Immediately, two men dashed from across the street, gathered Inspector Bloodstone under their arms, lifted him up and went running with him towards a horse and buggy that came around the corner at that moment.

James Moriarty

"For I have felt the pain of love, the depths of an agony that knows no bounds, and the heights of tremulous fame, and dare I say that I more than the great many have stood on the precipice of the ultimate achievement, only to see it thrust away from the safety of my feet and placed in the eager arms of the man whose cloth I dare not wear."

--From the Diary of James Moriarty.

221 B Baker Street

August 19, 1848. 7:01 pm

London, England

James stood at the window, looking out at the few pedestrians that walked past and the horse and buggies. Three of the newer electric cars whined past, their electric motors silent, but their transmissions a bit noisy.

One a shiny green with yellow lantern headlights. A second was one of the newer police wagons with a blue siren and red speakers on its sides.

The third was a grocery truck, topped with boxes of fresh apples from the South, and a tail gate with a hand painted image of Count Dracula and a quote, "Not all fangs are deadly to humans."

"Funny thing, Watson." James said after a time.

"What's that, James?" Watson said, after taking a sip of fresh juice, then setting it down on the table.

"How quickly science and technology seem to be advancing these days. Can remember as a child when there was no electricity, no electric cards, no aero planes and no blimps that crossed between continents."

"Your world maybe."

James grimaced. "Even after all these years I forget, I've become so merged with this blasted one. But it changes nothing the changes have been accelerating since I have been here. Even the steamers have become larger, more like floating palaces and faster. And the planes, noisy as they are, are so much faster than the older steamers."

"And thank God in heaven there are planes, my dear man, or we would be forever on those blasted boats, which smell like urine and rock a soul like it's never going to stop." Watson replied. "And besides earmuffs are much cheaper to purchase than nostril blockers, which strangle a man."

James laughed. "Still remember our last cruise, I take it?"

"I never want to travel to the North Pole again. Froze my bollocks off and was nearly eaten by that. That...that...that..."

"Apparition?" James asked, an amused look tickling his lips.

"Yes, and there was that as well. James, do you believe in the supernatural?"

"My dear friend, I believe in anything that is possible, is possible, and when it comes to our world, here and now, anything appears to be possible. And with our dear friend Tesla producing more and more inventions that defy the imagination, it can only be a matter of time before that dratted Edison fellow bests him and produces another idea that is stolen from him to benefit himself and not humanity."

"Take it you have no respect for Edison anymore then?"

"Oh no. I respect him. I just believe one should never turn ones back on him." James said with finality.

"Then why do he and Tesla still work together?"

James gave Watson a piercing look. "Some things are better not discussed about others."

"Oh." Watson said. "Oh!" He blurted next, catching on.

"Say, that's strange!" James said. He pushed the curtain back a bit to look more clearly at what was happening below their flat.

Watson got up to look. A horse and buggy were traveling past at a reckless pace. Two large burly men rode its sides and what looked like a newsboy rode its top, holding on for dear life.

"Someone rushing to the hospital?" Watson ventured.

"Which is the direction they are coming from." James pointed out.

Watson looked out. "Recognize the man driving. He was in the park when you and Good Queen Mary were talking."

James gathered his cloak and hat. "It looked like someone might need my help."

Watson threw on his cloak and hat. "You mean ours, do you not."

The two men rushed outside, with James limping a bit, but overcoming his pain to keep up with Watson, who suddenly remembered himself and slowed down. Watson spotted a horse and buggy across the street and back a bit. He blew a whistle, and the driver woke up. He had been nodding off after a long day of work and a bit of the nibble at a jug beside him. Which would explain his very red nose and cheeks and an eye that just kept quivering over and over as he spoke.

"Sirs?" The driver asked in a squeaky voice, perceiving a last drive and a big tip.

Watson climbed aboard, opened the door, and then reached a hand to his companion, who used his cane to help boost him inside.

Both men settled into opposite sides of the carriage.

Watson looked out. "After that horse and buggy, driver. And fast. There is a big tip in it for you!"

The Driver nodded his cap, and then urged his horses from the curb and quickly into a fast trot.

Inside the coach James's face was glowing. "As a friend of yours once said so excellently, 'The game's afoot,' Watson!"

The Invisible Man

"But James, there is no man above the law, nor greater than the law." As stated by Doctor Watson to his friend during the case of The Sniveling Coward Who Ate Children.

"True enough, dear Watson." James responded, *tapping his pipe to clear it of old ash. "But you must remember that laws are made by man, and not by the One True God whose laws are as far above man's comprehension, as man's laws are above those of the animals."*

--Snippet of a conversation held in Albert Hall during the trial of Doctor Frankenstein for the murder of Henry Talbot, the Wolf Man.

The Tower of London

July 21, 1849. 10:01 am

London, England

A very tall man with very round cheeks and a ruddy complexion, sweeps his cape over his right shoulder, and then pulled his deer cap lower over his forehead as he steps to the main entrance.

The building smells of salt and age, death, and contrition. Integrity and horror. A blend of the old and the new, the structure has been reinforced with self-healing metal that binds the old stone together. An invention of Doctor Pulitzer as atonement for his invention of bombs and the consequent deaths of many innocent lives during numerous wars.

A Royal Guard examines a document that the tall man hands over. Printed on a stiff leather with metal and gold embosses that have the royal coat of arms upon them: A Star with seven rays that contact seven other stars each with a lightning bolt through them against a sky of blue and purple. The Guard stiffened in honor to the man, then salutes and hands it back. He opens the old door, which is hoary with age and creaks and groans, like the tortured screams of those prisoners who had been held there in past decades and treated to monstrous inhumane actions.

The very tall man is met by another Royal Guard, whose shoulder holds a purple patch on it with the crown emblazoned on it, terribly like the Coat of Arms on the document viewed earlier. He examined the tall man's paper, nodded, and urged him onwards through a pair of large doors that opened onto a winding, spiral staircase that shot upwards.

The tower interior was more ripe smelling than even the exterior, smelling of sweat and blood, fear, and amusement of all things. The tall man mused upon that as he trod upwards. A place of such dark horrors and comedy. Only an enlightened being could make sense of such a contradiction, and he was not such, but he did believe that the comedy of it helped improve some of the disgusting history of its past.

The tall man did not slow down, even he appeared to have a limp of some kind when he took a step. His face showed brief bursts of discomfort as he strode ever upwards. But this man was tough. He faced far worse challenges and survived.

Finally, after what must have been an exceedingly long time for the soul, he stopped before a pair of doors emblazoned with the Royal Symbol...an eagle holding lightning bolts in its claws.

Two extremely tall Royal Guard of dark skin, holding very sharp sabers at salute stood left and right of the doors. An overweight, short man, who was obviously of the Court, sniffed into a hanky, then took the tall man's note. He read it quickly, nodded, and then urged the tall man through the double doors.

"Enter at your own risk, her majesty is in sorts this day."

The tall man ignored the caution and entered without hesitation.

The Court Clerk closed the doors behind him, blowing his nose loudly in his cotton handkerchief as he did.

The Tall man examined the chamber once more he stood within. A great window looked from the far right. The window curved and enclosed a thick, almost metallic glass that gave off numerous reflections as if polished and faceted on its faces like a diamond.

He could see merchant ships and military vessels winding their way up the Thames towards the Atlantic, past hoary, aged London and New London where the self-healing structures were being built increasingly often to replace the old. Again, a reminder of how different this world was from his last where age and history was respected and preserved, long past when they were necessary. He smiled. Necessity is the mother of invention as a good friend had once said and this world with its magic and constant military interventions certainly had much of the necessity.

His eyes flicked over the cold walls briefly, noting that everything was still in its proper place, except for the person he had come to see, who occupied an extremely comfortable chair that reclined and filled with soft silk cushions, her only submission to the comforts of wealth and nobility.

"Your Majesty." He greeted, inclining his head and half bowing to her as he did. He balanced slightly on his cane as he did so to keep from falling. He still had a way to go before his legs would so as he often commanded them to do in his efforts to rehabilitate himself.

Good Queen Mary of Scots rose from her lounge, which sat beside a blazing fireplace where fresh wood was neatly stacked. She came to him and lifted her hand, and he took it and lightly kissed it with his lips.

She smiled into his face; her soul radiant in her eyes. In his world she had been a proud woman who jailed and then beheaded by the guillotine by a jealous King, but in this one she had done that exact same thing. But in this world, the King did not get away with it. The people rose in rebellion and he was condemned for betraying the empire and its people.

"So good of you to come. Trust the climb was not too painful for you." She said, noting his slight limp.

He shrugged. "One must master the mortal coils of life, or it shall master them. Await your pleasure, your Majesty."

"Intend to master this infirmity then?"

He smiled. "To live in the sun, one must risk being burned."

"In that case I shall make sure you have plenty of sunlight." With those words she went to the left wall and pulled the beautifully embroidered red drapes there that hung from the ceiling, admitting the full light of day. The sunlight burst through

and lit the dark, old room filling it with bouncing rays of light.

She whirled around like a happy little girl might and then her face grew solemn as he gazed into her eyes, seeking what he knew she had been hiding in her earlier small talk.

"You know why I am here?"

She gestured him forward, showing a chair beside her royal table. She sat behind it as he sat down opposite her. She placed her silk sleeved arms upon the table and rested her chin upon her palms, gazing at him a long time, then she said slowly. Very slowly. "A strange thing on a strange day."

James at once stiffened. It was far worse than he had suspected. Was there time to stop it?

Oscar Wilde

"The sea has a great seducing force to it, my dear friend. And that is its ability to soothe even the wildest of nerves, to calm the beast within that rages to roar and defy death and to deny its roots in the divinity of all creatures."

--From the works of Oscar Wilde.

Thames Shipyard

July 21, 1849. 1:12 pm

London, England

A pair of rough and ready Sailors, fresh from shore leave, rubbed at bloodshot eyes and hurried up the plank to the freighter, whose main mast and top sails fluttered in the light breeze. The Tall Sailor had arms that looked as thick as trunks. He had built up quite a body over the years working with the heavy crates that their ship, "Potemkin," transported on regular voyages to and from the India Islands.

The Short Sailor was thin and ratty looking, his eyes never straying to one place for exceptionally long, but though he looked criminal, he was the most honest man on the boat. He shoved his cap back over his red hair, his brown eyes taking in the refreshing site above. It was demanding work, but it was his ship and his work.

They could see fellow Sailors climbing the ropes into the sails to fix tears and mend what could be saved or take down what could not be. They heard the roaring of men cursing as they stowed fresh cargo, their sweat rolling into hardened eyes. As they climbed a man, whose face was hid in a hood over his face, accidentally bumped into one of them.

"Hey!" Cried the Short Sailor and reached to grab the man.

The man dodged the grab.

Angered, the other Sailor dropped back to block his way. "A please I'm sorry as can be and begging for your forgiveness might

tempt your salvation, matey!"

Both Sailors rushed the man, but before they could make a move, the man moved so swiftly that their eyes could not follow the action and both Sailors were arcing off the plank into the salty waters on the sides.

The man looked down a moment, shook his head, and then continued down the ramp.

"Sir!" A voice came from above.

He stopped to look back.

A short, Chinese man, wearing the cottons of his trade and a headband of yellow cotton, hurried down the ramp, clutching a medical bag, which looked old and worn. "You forgot this in your cabin, Doctor."

The man took the bag, and then tipped the Chinese Man. All without a word of thanks, but the Chinese Man forgot the insult at once when his eyes saw just how big the tip was. He was all smiles as he returned to the kitchen, where he was helping a tall Swedish Cook with breakfast.

"You won't believe what I just got."

He showed the bank note he had been handed.

The Swedish Cook's eyes rounded like balloons. It was enough money to retire from the trade.

The Boar and Dragon

August 19, 1848. 3:02 pm.

London, England

"A beautiful woman is much like a wonderful diamond. It took many years for her to blossom and like a diamond, if mishandled, will crumble and perish from rough handling, but if adored, loved and carefully nurtured, shall surely be your best friend and companion through the years." A quote from Sir Nicolas Tesla when introducing Doctor Frankenstein to Mina Harker.

The horse and buggy with Inspector Bloodstone inside pulled around the side of the Boar and Dragon, an upper-class inn situated in lower London, where merchants and those with the means, would often come for play, as well as pleasure. Beautiful women hovered at the second level, surveying incoming men, and weighing up their odds for snatching one into the web of sensual pleasures they offered for insignificant change and a meal, hoping that one might be the one that became a steady client, or better yet, a ticket out of their lifestyle, which while legal, led nowhere as they aged.

The three men from the buggy carried Inspector Bloodstone to a door further to the right that was hidden be behind some stacks of crates, which slid aside easily as the smaller of them pressed a hidden release.

Once the barrels slid away the other two men carried the limp Lieutenant between them through a dark entrance with sputtering candles on the other side. The smaller man looked around to make sure no one was watching and closed the entrance, the barrels sliding noisily back into place.

Inspector Bloodstone was hauled through a short corridor where slabs of meat hung from hooks, past shelves filled with various brews and wines, then past a small kitchen where a dark man with a top knot of hair that shot upwards in a spiral of color, beat at meat with a huge cleaver.

He eyed the Lieutenant and raised his cleaver, as if wanting to add him to the meat he was tenderizing.

"Don't even think of it." The first of the men warned, as they continued through a thick curtain of cloth and hanging chains into the main tavern area. Not one patron turned an eye, or cared, for this place was the hub of not only pleasure and play, but of crime. The worst! Here, for a price, a common man could find sexual release or torture, depending upon his needs.

A merchant could find cargo at a reduced price with newly relabeled crates and sacks of stolen goods.

A jeweler might discover the rarest of diamonds, rubies, or sapphires fresh from Asia or the India Islands, Rescued from their rightful owners.

An assassin could search through wondrous drugs and herbs that would relinquish a life as easily as a thousand-foot drop to hard rocks below.

Yes, it was a terrible place and a place of wonder... for criminals.

The lack of attention stopped the moment the Tavern Master, who was the Master Criminal and Owner of the Inn, tromped from around the tavern bar, his eyes small and piercing, his cruel lips thin with anger and hatred.

The Tavern Master eyed Inspector Bloodstone as he passed and kicked him in the side. "That's for the last raid, you bugger! Cost me ten of my best men and a month's wages!"

Other men spit on Inspector Bloodstone as he passed, and another raised a knife to stab him but was stopped by the Tavern Master. "Even that man deserves some respect. For now!" He warned.

The man with the knife slunk off, but kept his eyes on Inspector Bloodstone, hoping for a later chance to enact his own retribution and vengeance upon the helpless soul. Such was the character of many within the tavern, which while brightly lit, with a blazing hearth, and light music from a piano player, still was a den of festering violence and decadence.

If the Lieutenant had been conscious at the time, he would have smelled death everywhere, for death happened in too many ways in that den of evil. Its smell was rank and foul. Its stench pervaded everything, but the men who lounged within the tavern reveled in it, wallowed in it, sought it...like the dark souls they were, they did not look for Light, but anything opposed to it.

The burly men took Inspector Bloodstone to a door. The one who had warned off the knife man earlier tapped on the door three times, then two, then once...

Nothing.

He repeated the tap again, this time louder, but with the taps in reverse.

The door made a loud, groaning sound as if its ancient hinges had not received a drop of oil since they were attached. A thick man stood on the other side. He had one eye and a black patch over the other with a scar that ran from his eyebrow down onto his cheek. His head was bald and had a tattoo of the devil upon it, with the demon's mouth eating a Sailor whose feet kicked helplessly from its mouth.

He wore thick diamond studs in both ears and a huge diamond ring on his left thumb.

His shirt was black, as were his cotton pants. He wore thick boots with hints of blood and something less savory as well.

"This him?"

"Aye." The man who had knocked responded.

The bald man looked over to the bar where the Tavern Master glanced back and made a slight nod.

He stepped aside and the two men dropped the Lieutenant to the floor, with no care for how he landed. Even unconscious, the Lieutenant cried out in pain.

The bald man took the Lieutenant by his hair and dragged him

into a dark and evil smelling room where huge unknown sea creatures lay bleeding their insides into buckets on either wall. The shorter man who had never been inside before, gasped in horror when he recognized the creatures for what they were Humans! Adults whose insides were exposed and skin missing.

They entered, and the door swung shut noisily behind them, to the sound of the shorter man throwing up.

About a minute later the tavern doors swung open and James and Watson strode inside.

"Your revolver?" James asked.

Watson patted his coat and James nodded.

They strode straight to the Tavern Master.

James placed a hundred-pound note on the bar and looked the Tavern Master in the eyes. "You have two choices. And I will only accept one of them."

Watson stepped back a bit, his eyes on the crowd, which while busy, had quietened when they walked in.

The Tavern Master kept wiping at the bar counter, ignoring James. "And what would those choices be?"

"The right one." James gestures to the note.

"And the one you don't want to choose." James finished.

The Tavern Master reached under the bar and strove to pull out a large knife, but James reached over and pinched the nerve in his neck.

The Tavern Master fell like a log.

Watson looked over at James with astonishment. "I've never seen anything like that?"

"Learned about it from a book I read of the Orient."

The Tavern dropped into instant silence.

Three big men rose to face Watson and James.

James turned to look, smiled, and put another hundred-pound note on the bar beside the first one. "One for each of you with the right answer."

The two men exchanged looked that were murderous. One of them glanced towards the door in the wall that the Inspector was taken through.

The Boar and Dragon

August 19, 1848. 3:22 pm.

London, England

"You harbor ill will and cultivate it in your heart like a good farmer tills his fields from dawn to dusk in hopes of a harvest, but the only crop your evil shall yield is the darkening of your soul and all hope of redemption and happiness in this life and the next." A quote from Pope Victorious to Baron Von Hitler before he trod on the blessed lands of the Papacy.

The hidden room was brighter now. Two wall lanterns had been lit. The Short Man stood to the back against the door, trying not to throw up again. He kept his eyes to the floor.

Before him, the second man stood to the right of the Bald Man who had Inspector Bloodstone on a bloody table with bits of meat still clinging to its sides and spills of blood and guts oozing down its sides.

The Bald Man had a very sharp knife in his fingers. He twirled it expertly, giving the others a crooked smile, revealing cannibalistic teeth that were as sharp as daggers. He tapped one.

"Tasted the finest," he finally replied, licking his lips in pleasure at the thought.

The other man, trying to be macho, and not show his shaking hands which were out of view behind his back, responded. "What do they taste like?"

The Bald Man put his blade to Inspector Bloodstone's jacket and cut it off with a bold sweep, then another sweep that took his shirt off, leaving a slight trail of blood across his chest.

"You really wanta know?" The Bald Man asked, peering at the other fellow.

The man nodded, afraid to say otherwise now that his overly enthusiastic remark had backfired on him.

The Bald Man raised his hand and started to bring it down towards the Lieutenant's nose. "Noses are the delicacy of such. Shall cut you a share of mine."

He continued his slice.

The Short Man at the back of the room cried out in alarm as the door flew inwards, knocking him screaming to the bloody floor, where he slid like ice across a slick floor and slammed into the heels of the Bald Man, who fell back before he could slice off the whole of Inspector Bloodstone's nose.

Watson strode inside with his pistol raised to fire.

The Bald Man fell back against a wall, still clutching his knife. The other man raised his hands at once.

"We're just having a little funs is all."

James stepped into the room, surveyed the body on the table and the three men.

"Where did you take him?"

Watson gave James a shocked look. "He's on the table, about to be butchered is where he is."

James shook his head and went to the body lying there that appeared to be Bloodstone's. He tugged at the bottom of the neck and lifted off an elaborate thick mask and tossed it aside.

"Bollocks!" Watson cried out.

James touched the blood on the man's chest. He raised it on a white gloved finger close to his eyes. "Congealed. At least ten hours now. This man's been dead for quite some time."

"You!" He pointed at the Bald Man.

"I didn't do it." He denied. "I just serve the meat is all."

Watson swung his pistol around to aim at the Bald Man's forehead. "Should put one between your eyes right now!"

James stepped back, keeping himself between the men and Watson. "He's right. He's just the butcher."

Watson did not lower his gun.

James dropped beside him. "We're too late."

The smaller man on the floor groaned, then sat up, rubbing his head. "What hit me..." He stopped when he saw the gun and the taller men at the door. His eyes widened in horror. He tried to get to his feet, but the blood kept him losing his balance.

Finally, he gave up. He pointed a shaking finger at James. "You're that...that...detective fellow. Sherlock Holmes!"

Watson grimaced but said nothing.

James noticed but turned away to look at the smaller man.

"Would you like to earn some money?"

The smaller man gave James a look of utter confusion.

James Moriarty

"Once I transitioned to the new world, I began to realize that not only did our two worlds differ in substance, but also in quality. Human motives stayed the same, but for some reason this world had heroes of extraordinary quality, like Sherlock Holmes, and Professor Langston, the Invisible Man. In our world they would have been fairy tales or stories of a literature kind, but here they were living, breathing flesh made real. And science was pacing forward at a remarkable rate as if it could never stop. It's almost as if the Creator had loosed all stops here to see what Its creations would become." ---

--From the journals of James Moriarty.

The Boar and Dragon

August 19, 1848. 3:32 pm.

London, England

James stepped into the main tavern room. Behind him in the tavern, a number of men lay on the floor groaning, or quiet, while others milled around anxiously, panicked, and unsure what to do next.

James pocketed the two noted he had laid on the bar counter, and then shut the door behind them.

Watson glanced at him. "How come you never offer me any choices like that?"

"Friends don't bribe friends, Watson."

"So now what? If they haven't murdered him yet, then they soon may." Watson said.

"Had they wished him dead, our butcher in the back would already be carving on him."

"Disgusting creature, you should have let me finish him."

"What and discolor your good name forever?"

"How so? Would be ridding the world of a monster."

"In a world of monsters even the monsters have their place. Water seeks its own level. Believe me when I say he will find a path that leads to his redemption. If not now, then later."

"But he was carving up that poor man."

"Who had died of the very thing we seek to stop."

"But why would he eat him?"

"Perhaps for the same reason madmen do many things. To see what the results would be."

James had his eye on the portrait of Captain Blackbeard that hung behind the bar. It hung over a heavily wooded wall.

"Watson, do check the rim of that painting closer for me."

"Why me? You have the magnifying glass."

James pulled out a broken glass. "It broke when I smashed the door down."

"Humph!" Watson said, and then went to the portrait of Her Majesty. "See fingerprints on the side of the frame."

"Bravo, Watson, I knew you could do it." James said, joining Watson.

"Well then." James said with a grin. "Do the honors."

Watson shoved the portrait to the right. Nothing happened. He grunted, and then shoved the portrait to the left. Still nothing happened. Finally, he tried to lift it from the wall.

The back wall made a loud, groaning sound and opened into a lantern lit stairwell that descended into darkness.

"After you." James said.

"What about these beasts behind us?"

The smaller man came out of the back room with his friend and the Bald Man. They all held clubs in their hands.

"Oh. I don't think they'll be any problem now."

Watson arched an eyebrow, grunted, then

Watson grunted. "Why don't you go first this time?"

"Because you have the weapon." James said pleasantly, closing the wall behind them as they stepped into the stairwell.

And not too soon, as the tavern door opened and a storm of men with knives burst inside. They milled around, confused for a moment, as they saw all the groaning men laying on smashed tables and, on the floor, trying to move, but still unable to.

They looked at each other as if a ghost had gotten away from them and they had fallen into the pits of hell, but hell was not on the floor, but on the faces of the three men with clubs who were walking towards them with evil gleams in their eyes.

How could things possibly get any worse?

One of the men smiled at Watson. "Like the fats ones, so much juicier." Then he licked his lips in anticipation.

Albert Einstein

"The depths of man's depravity can reach no further than the heights of his folly, but the zenith of a man's enlightenment is immeasurable, glorious and as brilliant as the nearest star."

--A quote from Albert Einstein's Instances of Man's Behavior and Enlightenment through Self Physics.

Canal beneath The Boar and Dragon

August 19, 1848. 3:48 pm.

London, England

Inspector Bloodstone was handed down the last step of a wet and slimy quay onto a narrow boat with three men, two aft, and one fore with shipped oars. As soon as Inspector Bloodstone was placed into the middle of the boat by the two burly men managing him, the boat men unshipped their oars and prepared to embark.

The two burly men nodded to them and turned back to the staircase they had come down. The first one climbed five steps, and then mysteriously came flying back down, tumbling into the other one behind him.

Both men fell onto the quay and lay there, stunned.

The crew of the boat was confused at first, but when James stepped out, brushing off his white gloved hands, with Watson just to his side aiming his pistol at the crew of the boat, all became instantly clear.

James stepped forward and gently turned over the first of the burly men. His face was bloody all over it, his eyes open and staring at the ceiling above.

He turned over the second burly man and his head fell to the side like the broken appendage it had become. Blood was spilling from both his ears and nostrils.

Watson kept his gun on the boat crew.

"Dead, are they?"

"Singing with the angels," James said. He gently closed both men's eyes, then turned to look at Watson.

"Oh, I don't think the place where they're going to, there's going to be much singing." Watson said with a note of satisfaction.

"Look her, Watson, a man might be evil on this turn of the wheel, but there is other turned to come, and he could become a saint!"

"Oh balderdash, James. Enough of your sanctimonious spirituality. We've got three men to bring to justice and an unconscious Lieutenant to save."

James sighed, and then headed for the boat.

He only got three paces from the boat when all three men began coughing and heaving, as if choking on something. All three men opened their mouths and a stream of blood flowed out. All three men flailed their arms in the air, then slumped over the railing of the boat...dead.

"Most peculiar." Watson said, his eyebrows narrowing.

"Indeed, good Watson. Indeed." James agreed.

James stooped over the first dead burly man and swabbed a stub of cotton in his blood, then put it into a small vial from his cape.

He and Watson took Inspector Bloodstone from the boat as carefully as they could, and with great difficulty began making their way back up the stairwell.

Once they had re-entered the Tavern above and shut the door behind them a figure in the shadows stepped into view. His face was invisible in the gloom of a hood over his head and eyes. The figure went to the quay, examined both bodies there, then the ones in the boat. It was the Tall Man from the ship.

He took out a series of bottles from his medical bag and began taking samples from the various men. Finished, he took a large flask from his medical bag, and then began sprinkling it over the boat and the two fallen men.

He stepped back, and then lit a match. He flung it, and then fell back into the shadows as the quay exploded into flames.

Good Queen Mary

"I imagine that if every man were as diligent as you, then there would be no stone unturned and no life unsaved. That our world would be a bright light onto the Universe to see and that the Angels would sing in delight."

--Good Queen Mary of Scots words of endearment to her best friend.

July 21, 1849. 12:01 pm.

James followed Inspector Bloodstone as the man swaggered towards the site of the fallen man. "And it's totally by accident that I found out about this."

"I say, it usually is, dear Inspector Bloodstone." James agreed.

Inspector Bloodstone gave him a grin and then grimaced. "Ouch, you surely know how to crush a man's spirit."

"Nonsense. You thrive on diversity. You are armored by your self-assurance and your ability to hide the facts from themselves."

Inspector Bloodstone did not know whether to look insulted or complimented, so decided to do neither and go ahead towards the crime scene, followed by Watson at a discrete distance, who was looking for clues and from time to time dropping to a knee to examine the soil. "So, what does our brave crime fighter take from this latest incident?" James asked.

Inspector Bloodstone stopped before a covered body, draped by a thick burlap sack. A farmer stood nearby, keeping his horse steady, its nerves a bit frayed by the electric car that had pulled up with Inspector

Bloodstone, James, and Watson.

"It seems that his death has no known cause."

James tossed the burlap back to reveal the man's body and the blood there. Watson started to reach down to touch the blood, but James stopped him.

"I wouldn't."

"And why not?" Watson asked.

"Because this man is contagious." James said, turning to eye a Constable who had been guarding the body.

The Constable was sweating extremely in the chilly air, shivering at the same time, and his eyes were beginning to tear small droplets of blood.

Inspector Bloodstone crossed himself. "God have mercy!"

"He has if you have not touched this man." James declared.

Inspector Bloodstone hastily stepped back.

Watson turned to James. "But you have just touched the burlap that was upon his body. And the farmer seems healthy enough."

"True, Watson. Astute observations. But note these things. First the farmer would have already been dead by now had he actually touched the body. He only covered it, and carefully, I dare say."

James nodded. "As to the Constable I suspect, dear Inspector Bloodstone, if you examine his pants, you will find the ring that is missing from the index finger of our fallen man here."

Inspector Bloodstone swung on the Constable, who hastily turned about and ran off. Inspector Bloodstone started after him, but James stopped him. "Don't. He is already a dead man. One. Two...."

The Constable gasped loudly, grabbed at his eyes, and then collapsed into a huddle, his eyes streaming blood.

"This is monstrous," Inspector Bloodstone said.

"Truly." Watson said. "Such a horrid disease is unheard in these modern days and times."

"No, I meant a Constable robbing a dead man." Inspector Bloodstone said.

"As opposed to taking their personal items while they are alive?" James asked gently.

Inspector Bloodstone turned on him. "Whatever are you talking about?"

James pointed to a lump in Inspector Bloodstone' right pocket. Inspector Bloodstone emptied it, revealing a diamond ring. "I found it at the Tavern upon the Master. Bringing it in for examination and evidence."

James turned away the same time as he cleared his throat, leaving the Lieutenant blushing a bright red and deeply humiliated.

Watson did his best not to snicker, by turning away and heading back for the electric car.

"Coming?" He tossed over his shoulder.

"In a moment." James answered, stooping. He took out a small veil and a tab of cotton. He smeared a part of the cotton with blood from the dead man, and then shoved the cotton into the vial.

As he rose, he saw something peculiar. He stooped closer and then began scribbling furiously in a small notebook he took out of his right cape pocket. He finished, and then rose to follow Watson, who was climbing into the electric car behind Inspector Bloodstone.

Doctor Watson

"My only regret during my short tenure in this magical world of humanity is that I cannot find an ounce of forgiveness for my nemesis, nor forgiveness in my own heart for wanting and craving it." From a conversation with Doctor Watson who mentioned what James had felt after the plunge from Reichenbach Falls that had killed the archnemesis and left him crippled for years.

Tower of London

July 21, 1849. 3:45 pm.

London, England

Watson stood at attention beside Inspector Bloodstone, and James as the Good Queen Mary stood before them. Several Royal Guards stood at the doors behind them.

"So, what is so important that you interrupt my meeting with the heads of state of three different countries clamoring to war with us?"

James inclined his head. "Solved the case."

Inspector Bloodstone and the Good Queen Mary, both gave him perplexed looked. Watson merely watched. He was used to the astounding leaps of logic his companion often made, even though he felt a bit strange, as he could not remember there being any recent case.

"Proceed." The Good Queen Mary said with the hint of a smirk on her rosy cheeks.

James inclined his head again. "As you know in 1848 at The Boar and Dragon and later on in several dozen other places, men of nobility and merchants, as well as several famous officers of the court died in a very mysterious manner."

"Even our dear Inspector Bloodstone seemed on course for a similar death." James explained. "Though the fact that he survived when no one else had remains a mystery till now."

The Good Queen Mary fidgeted with her royal ring, twisting it nervously about her index finger. "Go on."

She glanced at the Lieutenant who looked extremely uncomfortable and embarrassed but gave no clue what he was thinking at that moment, even though his heart, if the truth be known, were in a great turmoil.

"The loss of so many citizens would be hard to forget, considering the panic it caused throughout England and Europe for that matter." She finally said, responding to James' earlier remark.

"Indeed." James answered. "Which is why it is so pertinent now to what happened at Stonehenge this day and at Hornsley Street, both to men of substance and fame, though some of it might be a bit dubious."

The Good Queen Mary's face grew beet red. "I say that the Lord Honor Justice Herrington was hardly a man of dubious fame."

"Quite the contrary." James went on, oblivious to the growing wrath of the Good Queen Mary. Her guards had noticed her displeasure, and were edging closer, hands on their swords.

Watson began to sweat. This could be unbelievably bad. Bad indeed.

"You see." James said, pulling out a vial he had taken earlier in the day at Stonehenge. "This vial contains a virus so virulent that the slightest contact means death."

He opened the vial and poured its contents upon his palm.

Everyone backed away from him, fearing the worst, except for Watson, who bravely stood his ground.

"I found it extremely odd that Lieutenant Bloodstone should be in direct contact with both the men who died from this virus, as well as the boatmen on the ship. Yet here he stands, hale and hearty, smart and wise as ever."

Watson had to hide a snicker at that, which the Good Queen Mary caught and gave him a scathing glance for, to which he promptly returned a look of utter innocence.

"But there is no virus after all, but rather a chemical that has been imported from India. A Vedic chemical that when combined with certain other elements, such as salt water...or a certain kind of dust, turn it into a violently destructive weapon that ravages the immune system and our red blood cells."

James put the vial to his lips and sipped from it, swallowing

the cotton swab within it.

The Good Queen Mary's face turned pale as a ghost.

James turned to look at Inspector Bloodstone. "Suspect you can explain the rest." He nodded to the Royal Guards, and they moved forward and clasped Inspector Bloodstone by his elbows.

"Protest." Inspector Bloodstone said loudly.

"And well you should." James answered, and then looked at

the ambassador standing behind the Good Queen Mary, who had been observing everything quietly, thinking he was unnoticed.

"Seize that man!" James ordered.

The Royal Guard released Inspector Bloodstone, who sagged with relief, then rushed to detain the Ambassador, who tried to get away.

The Ambassador groaned angrily. "What is this nonsense?"

"Oh, nonsense indeed." James agreed amiably. "Let

him go. Here, before us, stands the true culprit, wearing the divine face of innocence."

The Royal Guard the Ambassador loose. He brushed off where they had touched, his whiskered cheeks puffed out like a porcupine in anger. "So, you have eliminated everyone, but Doctor Watson beside you."

James looked at Doctor Watson, who paled.

"Surely, you don't suspect I would do such a dastardly thing?"

The Royal Guards looked at Doctor Watson, eager to follow through, but James waved them off. The Ambassador grunted angrily. "Then has this whole discussion been a charade, a shakedown to elicit a poor kind of humor from us with your cowardly suspicions?"

"Not at all." James answered honestly, his eyes not on the Ambassador, but on the Good Queen Mary, who now looked like a deer caught in the headlight of an oncoming car collision.

"But..." He paused for dramatic effect, then sighed. "Suspect she will not be so willing to take arrest."

Everyone turned to look at the Good Queen Mary, whose face turned horribly angry and ugly. "How dare you accuse me of such common acts of murder? I am the enlightened ruler of this nation, not a mass murderer!"

"Indeed." James purred gently, his voice becoming more soothing, but also sterner at the same time.

"Your Majesty has a history of vanishing for some time into India, in the more uncharted areas. And it is also a well-known fact that before you ascended the throne through our late and beloved King Charles, that you had a tremendous knowledge of chemicals and biology. Hence the deduction I forthwith give. You have been using this rare element from the Vedas to first seduce, then destroy those who appeared to aide and assist you."

Inspector Bloodstone paled.

James turned to eye the man. "And you, sir, do you still feel so free to defend your vow of silence?"

Even as Inspector Bloodstone began choking with uncertainty, the Good Queen Mary sighed, and then slumped into her chair.

"Must confess."

Everyone relaxed but tensed when she clutched at the ornamental dagger at her side. "It was I. But for good reason."

She looked up. "There has been a great conspiracy known only to me and a few others, all of whom are dead now and unable to support me in this."

"And what conspiracy would that be?" James asked, knowing that this was the decisive moment. Enlightenment for all.

"That there has been a grand deception of the sort that defies imagination. That our country, our world has been invaded by a most heinous and dark soul." She went on.

She looked up at James. "Don't you see? Were I to reveal what I had found out; their plot would have succeeded. England would be theirs. Germany. France. The Italias. The India Islands. All of it! But I have single handedly destroyed their henchmen, thus saving our world from a crisis beyond imagination."

As she continued to confess, Watson noted several Doctors, he knew well from the London Hospital, stepped into the room from the corridor outside. Their faces were grim and troubled. They stopped just behind the Royal Guard.

Then Watson remembered where he had seen them. They were specialists in abnormal psychology. Watson felt a tremendous amount of sympathy for the Good Queen Mary at that moment, knowing what she must surely face next.

The Good Queen Mary did not see them. Her eyes

were on her ceremonial dagger.

"But there's more." She went on.

"I think that the one who instigated this invasion is still at large in our country. He is well known and well respected and so far, untouchable. By me or even James."

She rose and then noted the Doctors. She smiled. "So, it's to be this way then?"

The Ambassador cleared his throat. "We truly apologize for the deception but found it necessary to discover the truth."

"Much of which yet remains hidden. Is this not true, your Majesty?" James asked.

She turned her eyes towards him. They were streaming tears. "I have trusted you with my life."

"And it's a trust well earned. For your protection we do what we must now." He said gently. But before she left, she stopped before him and offered her hand. He took it and gently pressed his lips to her ring.

"Will always be in your debt, your Majesty." He said, simply and with care.

"Know." She said in a mysterious voice, and then departed with the two Royal Guards and Doctors beside her.

Watson turned to James. "Confused. There appears to be no villain here at all."

"Truthfully, there are many here, but because the evil done has been done in the name of saving many, much will be hidden and remain hidden." James confessed sadly.

James looked at Inspector Bloodstone. "Some who are not so innocent require some time to think about what they have chosen to do as their part of this conspiracy against conspiracies."

"Others." He turned to look at Watson. "Others may find it best to forgive later on, what they understood not before."

And with those mysterious words, he left the room and a mystified Watson.

The Tower of London

July 21, 1849. 5:05 pm.

London, England

James and Watson exited the front door, followed by Inspector Bloodstone, who gave them a nod and went to his electric car to drive off.

James turned to Watson and smiled into the setting sun. "What a great night this shall be. Shall we celebrate?"

"Celebrate what?" Watson asked, totally mystified by his companions' demeanor. "I feel nothing, but great tragedy has befallen our evening. Dark and cold it is in my heart."

"Oh, come on, Watson, now you're beginning to sound like that William fellow with all his plays."

"Shakespeare is a nobleman and a gentleman." Watson rebuffed.

"That remains to be seen." James said mysteriously.

"So why celebrate? The Good Queen Mary has been deposed...."

"No... not deposed...taken to safety."

Watson turned about to give James a look of utter astonishment. "Good lord, man, I saw her carted off myself to the looney bin."

"Watson, not all that is visible..."

"Yes, I know...is necessarily the truth. But what does that have to do with..."

Watson's eyes rounded again. "My God! You have sent her to safety!"

"Yes. And a dubious one at that, for the evil she suspected looms darkly still over our realms, but until we must face that evil more directly, I suggest we celebrate this night for the glorious moment in our befuddled existences as we can."

"Suppose you're right." Watson grumbled, turning to the sidewalk, which he began walking down.

"And we can be grateful we're alive. Alive and able to change the course of our destinies, minute by minute, hour by hour, day by day and if we're truly lucky, year by year."

On those odd words he took his cane from beside the door and limped off with a befuddled Watson following several paces behind.

The setting sun cast gentle golden fingers of light across both men, showering them and their shadows with warmth.

Unseen by both men was the stranger with the

hooded face. He stood about twenty faces back, watching. Watching.

"James."

"Yes, John."

"You still haven't explained everything."

"I know."

"And?"

"All good things in their time, Doctor Watson. All good things in their time."

Pope Alexander the Great

"It is said that every story has a beginning, middle and an end, but is it just possible that all beginnings, middles and ends are so closely intertwined that they are ceaselessly changing and evanescently curious in the way they play out in the humor psyche? Perhaps we are so focused on the ending of it all, that we miss out on the Greater Continuity that binds us all together."

--James's confession to the late Pope Alexander the Great.